# Ki.... Valentine Cookies

## Book Five

## in

## Killer Cookie

## Cozy Mysteries

## By

## Patti Benning

**Author's Note:**  On the next page, you'll find out how to access all of my books easily, as well as locate books by best-selling author, Summer Prescott. I'd love to hear your thoughts on my books, the storylines, and anything else that you'd like to comment on – reader feedback is very important to me. Please see the following page for my publisher's contact information. If you'd like to be on her list of "folks to contact" with updates, release and sales notifications, etc…just shoot her an email and let her know. Thanks for reading!

Also…

…if you're looking for more great reads, from me and Summer, check out the Summer Prescott Publishing Book Catalog:

http://summerprescottbooks.com/book-catalog/ for some truly delicious stories.

**Contact Info for Summer Prescott Publishing:**

Twitter: @summerprescott1

Blog and Book Catalog:
http://summerprescottbooks.com

Email: summer.prescott.cozies@gmail.com

And…look up The Summer Prescott Fan Page on Facebook – let's be friends!

If you're an author and are interested in publishing with Summer Prescott Books – please send Summer an email and she'll send you submission guidelines.

# TABLE OF CONTENTS

# KILLER VALENTINE
# COOKIES

**Book Five in Killer Cookie Cozy Mysteries**

# CHAPTER ONE

L ilah Fallon slid two heart-shaped sugar cookies into a paper bag and folded the top over before handing it to her customer. "Thanks for shopping at The Casual Cookie. Come again soon!"

She watched the young woman leave, feeling a deep sense of satisfaction. It had been over a year since the cookie shop's grand opening, and it seemed as if each day was better than the last. It was hard to imagine that she had been almost paralyzed with doubt the year before. True, many of her new career ideas had ended in disaster, but it seemed that she had finally found something that would stick… as least as far as a job went.

Sighing, Lilah glanced down at her phone, which was sitting on the counter next to the register. There were three people she was aching to speak to, but she couldn't turn to any of them. First was her father, who had collapsed the week before and was now lying in a hospital bed hours away while his doctors struggled to figure out what went wrong. Next was Reid, her boyfriend — sort of — who had taken their relationship to a standstill after their last date. And finally, there was Margie.

Lilah felt guilt well up inside her at the thought of her friend. She had borrowed Margie's car the week before to go visit her father when he had first been admitted to the hospital, knowing that her own little beat up car would never make it. She had been on the phone with her mother when, out of nowhere, a dog had leapt into the road. She had swerved, totaling the car and giving herself a nasty bruise on the forehead that still hadn't completely faded.

Margie had handled the incident with grace, but Lilah knew that things still weren't right between them — and wouldn't be until she paid her friend back for the damages. She would never be able to look the older woman in the eye without wanting to crawl under a rock until she had fixed the mess that she had made.

The bell at the front of the shop rang as a little boy pushed the door open, his mother trailing behind him. Lilah recognized these customers, and beamed at the boy, pushing her personal issues to the back of her mind for the time being.

"Hey, Tommy. How'd you do?" she asked.

"Great," he said, proudly holding up a paper with a big, red letter A at the top. "I spelled all of the words right, and even got the bonus word."

"Good job," she said. "I guess that means you get a cookie, right?" She glanced up at his mother, not wanting to overstep her boundaries.

"Yep, choose any cookie you want, Tommy. You earned it."

Lilah felt her heart glow as she watched the little boy carefully examine every cookie in the display case before finally settling on a giant chocolate chunk cookie with a scoop of ice cream on top. She put the cookie on a plate, then went into the kitchen to scoop the ice cream on top and grab the two sodas his mother had asked for, then watched as they sat down at one of the little tables and the boy dug in with a thrilled expression on his face. *This is what I do*, she thought. *I make people happy, and somehow, I'm actually making a living doing it.*

The door opened, and another couple of customers came in, a man and woman holding hands. She greeted them cheerfully, then waited while they examined the cookies. The woman, who had beautiful long blonde hair that Lilah was envious of, couldn't seem to stop smiling.

"What should I get?" she asked.

"You can't go wrong here, Mariah. This place has wonderful cookies."

Lilah felt a warm glow in her heart at that. Just a few seconds later, another man came in and began to look over the photos on the wall, waiting his turn. Lilah beamed. She loved seeing the cookie shop so busy. She glanced at the clock, still trying to make sense of the ebb and flow of business. She had heard other business owners talking about their busy hours, but still hadn't seen much of a pattern at the cookie shop.

A moment later she heard Tommy's mother exclaim and looked over just in time to see Tommy reach across the table and accidentally knock his soda over with his elbow. His mother jumped up, but Lilah waved her back.

"I'll take care of it in just a second," she said. "And I'll grab you another soda, too. Don't worry about it."

She bagged the creamy mint chip cookies the man and woman had chosen, then stepped out from around the counter to grab a roll of paper towels from the bathroom. She only made it a few steps away, however, when she heard someone shout, followed by a loud crash.

"What happened?" she asked, hurrying back to the front. "Are you okay?"

The man was on the floor, rubbing the back of his head and looking dazed. "I… uh, I think so. I was walking around the spill, but I think I stepped on a piece of ice."

"We're so sorry," Tommy's mother said. "I should have just cleaned it up right away."

"It's not your fault," Lilah said. "I'm the one who told you to wait. Are you sure you're okay, sir? Do you need help getting up?"

"No, no, I'm fine," he said. "Don't worry, I'm not going to sue you." He gave a dry chuckle. "Goodness knows I don't need the money. A little bump on my head couldn't wreck this sort of day." Lilah smiled hesitantly, not quite sure what he was talking about.

"At least let me get you a free cookie for your troubles. Go ahead and choose whatever you'd like on the house, and I'll get started on cleaning up this mess."

After Tommy and his mother left, Lilah took advantage of the fact that the shop was empty and went into the kitchen to drink a cold glass of water and try to calm down. She knew that it was bad that the man had slipped. He had said he wasn't going to sue her, but what if he changed his mind? It could be the end of The Casual Cookie. She certainly didn't have hundreds of thousands of dollars just lying around to pay off a lawsuit. He had *seemed* okay. He had gotten up and walked out of the store with no issue. She just hoped it didn't come back to bite her in the future. She ran a business now, she had to be more careful about things like that. A spilled drink was a hazard, not just an inconvenience.

"Calm down," she told herself. "There's no reason to worry. I need to stop getting so worked up."

The past couple of weeks had been so horrible, and she had really begun leaning on the store for support. She had buried herself in her work, and even when the cookie shop was closed, she spent a lot of time in the kitchen baking and trying out new recipes. If she lost The Casual Cookie on top of everything else, what would she do?

The bell out front rang, and Lilah gathered herself, pushing the panic away and forcing herself to smile. Worrying wouldn't get her anywhere, and right now her job was to brighten another person's day with a delicious premium cookie or two.

# CHAPTER TWO

Even though the town of Vista, Alabama was nestled just an hour from the coast, it was still chilly enough out that evening that Lilah was glad she had remembered to bring her jacket with her when she left for work that morning. She had insisted that Margie use her car, which meant that she was stuck walking to and from work. It was dark out by the time she closed the cookie shop for the day, but there were still enough Christmas lights left up that her walk home wasn't too bad. She loved seeing the decorations, even if Christmas had been the month before.

With her hands in her pockets and her jacket zipped up, she started off down the sidewalk, feeling sorry for herself. Everything seemed to be going wrong lately. All of her relationships were a mess, her father was in the hospital, and now she had this new problem to worry about. No one had ever gotten injured at The Casual Cookie before, and on top of her concern about getting sued, she also felt guilty.

*It's almost Valentine's Day*, she thought as she walked along. *Reid and I had plans. Now he's not even talking to me.* She kicked at a pebble, knowing that she was being childish, but unable to help it. It made it worse that everything other than her father's illness was her own fault. She was the one who had crashed Margie's car, and it had been her who hadn't cleaned up the spilled drink in the cookie shop right away. She was the one who had freaked out when Reid had told her that he loved her.

*I can't seem to stop messing up my life.* Ever since she had opened The Casual Cookie, she had been so happy. She had proven to everyone that she had been right to strike out on her own and get away from the family business. Before the cookie shop, she had gone through a rough patch that had made her doubt her own choices and abilities, though she had kept up a cheerful face to everyone else.

Now, she was once again wondering if she had what it took to be independent. She couldn't seem to stop making mistakes. She had a long line of failures to look back on. Was The Casual Cookie just going to be one more to add to her list?

By the time she reached her front door, she was in a dark mood. She had forgotten to turn on the outdoor lights before she left that morning, so she had to fumble for the right key in the dark. When she opened the door, she was greeted by Winnie, her beagle, who urgently had to go outside. Lilah stood in the doorway, watching as the dog sniffed around the front yard. At least she had two beings in her life that were always there for her; Winnie, and her cat, Oscar. Their company was priceless to her. She just wished that she could be there for them more. The cookie shop was open six days a week, with Monday being her only day off. She didn't have any employees, so whenever the shop was open, she was there. That meant that she was gone a lot, and Winnie and Oscar spent a lot of time alone.

"Are you all done?" she asked the beagle as she came trotting back to the door with her tail wagging. "Let's go inside and get you some dinner."

By the time she had scooped food into the dog's and cat's food bowls, given them fresh water, and sorted through the day's mail, she was feeling more like herself. The incident at the cookie shop probably wasn't a big deal. The man *had* said he wasn't going to sue her, and he had seemed perfectly fine when he left. She was still worried about her father, but she knew that if his condition had worsened, her mother would have called. She was sure she would figure things out with Reid and Margie... eventually. Right now, she was hungry. She had fed her pets, and now it was time for her own dinner.

She checked the fridge, but what she found inside was not promising. She wanted something warm and hearty, not another cold deli meat and cheese sandwich. With a sigh, she shut the refrigerator door and walked over to the pantry. *Hmm,* she thought. *Potatoes, onions, garlic, and I saw heavy cream and some shredded cheese in the fridge. I think I have all the ingredients to make some cheesy potato soup. If that isn't comfort food, I don't know what is.*

She knew that cooking the potatoes would be the thing that took the longest, so she chopped them into small squares before putting them into the pot of water to boil. While she waited for that to happen, she got out all of the other ingredients, and looked up a recipe online to make sure she wasn't missing anything. When she saw a recipe for Beer Cheese Soup, she grinned. It just so happened she had the last two beers from a six-pack in the back of her fridge. It hadn't been a great day, and she figured she deserved a treat. Her dinner might not exactly be healthy, but it would be good.

Just under an hour later, she settled down on the couch with a large bowl of steaming hot soup in front of her, and the second bottle of beer on the coffee table. The rest of the soup was cooling on the stove, and there was enough left for her dinner the following day. She pulled a blanket onto her lap and set the bowl down before turning on the television. Once she found a program to watch, she grabbed her spoon and took the first taste of her creation. It was wonderful.

"None for you," she said, as Winnie jumped up on the couch. "Remember what happened last time you ate something with cheese in it?"

The dog was undeterred, and continued to gaze at her hopefully. Lilah bit back a laugh, not wanting to encourage the beagle, and turned her attention back to the television while she finished her meal. It was the perfect end to a not-so-perfect day. After eating, she would go and wash the few dishes in the sink, then she could get started on a new batch of homemade dog biscuits. Running The Casual Cookie might keep her away from home more, but it did have some benefits for her pets. She loved to try new healthy recipes for treats for them, and had even begun to sell some of the pet cookies in her shop. People loved their pets, and were eager to buy locally made, healthy treats for them.

She was just finishing up her last spoonful of soup when someone knocked at the front door. She froze, the spoon halfway to her mouth. "Winnie, come back," she hissed as the dog took off for the kitchen. Putting the bowl down on the coffee table, she rose and tiptoed over to the living room window. By pulling the curtains aside and pressing her face to the window, she could just see the front stoop, and the person standing on it.

Margie. Lilah bit her lip. Her dear friend. Before the incident with the car, Lilah would have gladly opened the door and let the other woman in. The two of them would have gossiped and laughed together while they baked, and Lilah could have told the older woman all of her worries. Now, however, she knew that she couldn't face an evening with her friend. She wouldn't be able to look at Margie without feeling like she wanted to crawl into a hole and hide. She knew that until she found a way to fix her friend's car, she wouldn't be able to fix things between the two of them.

With a sigh, she pulled the curtain shut and sat down on the couch. Margie knocked one last time, then there was silence.

# CHAPTER THREE

The next morning, Lilah woke up feeling groggy and unhappy. She had stayed up too late the night before, torturing herself by watching romance movies. The weather matched her spirits; cold rain was pelting down, and every once in a while, a gust of wind strong enough to rattle the shingles came along, making the rain go wild. Her mood was only worsened by the knowledge that she had to walk to the cookie shop in this weather.

*If only Val was in town*, she thought. *I could ask her for a ride.* Valerie Palmer had been her best friend since college, and was usually the person that Lilah turned to whenever her life took a turn for the worse, but the other woman was currently on a three-week-long winter cruise with her own family. She had been invited to go along, but hadn't wanted to close down The Casual Cookie for so long. Now, she was beginning to wish she had accepted the invitation.

"Maybe it will lighten up by the time I have to leave," she said aloud. "I'm bound to have good luck at some point."

She tore herself away from the window and left the bedroom, switching on the TV as she walked through the living room to the kitchen, where she filled the tea kettle with water and put it on a burner. Calling Winnie over, she opened the front door.

"Go on out," she said. The dog looked up at her mournfully. "I know it's raining, but there's nothing I can do about that. Are you going to hold it all day?"

Her tail tucked between her legs and her head drooping, Winnie slowly set one paw after the other down and made her way out the door, down the stoop, and onto the grass where she relieved herself before dashing back inside. By now, the tea kettle was whistling, so Lilah got a bowl out of the cupboard, dumped a packet of maple and brown sugar oatmeal in it, and poured the hot water into the bowl. While she waited for the oatmeal to soak, she grabbed a scoop of cat food and went into the living room to dump it into Oscar's bowl on the windowsill.

"An update on the man found in Vista earlier this morning. He passed away shortly after arriving at Alabama Memorial Hospital. His next of kin has been contacted, and the police are currently working to find out what happened to him. If you saw this man in or near Vista, Alabama yesterday evening, possibly with a head injury, please call the number at the bottom of the screen."

Lilah glanced at the TV automatically, then did a double-take. The man in the picture was the one who had slipped and fallen at the cookie shop the day before. "Oh, my goodness," she breathed.

The cat food scoop fell out of her hand, and she slid down the wall, hugging her knees to her chest as she stared at the screen from the floor. *Possibly with a head injury...* The words seemed to echo in her head. What had she done? Had this poor man died from the fall? It didn't make sense; he had seemed perfectly fine when he left, and she hadn't thought that he had hit his head very hard. And what had happened to the woman who had been with him? Why hadn't she insisted he go to the doctor if he had been acting oddly?

*They didn't say that he died from a head injury, just that he had one*, she thought. She forced herself to take a couple of deep breaths. He could have died from something else — a car crash, a heart attack, or he could even have been attacked by someone. She needed to learn more before she started to panic.

Muting the TV, which had switched to a commercial, she grabbed her laptop from her bedroom and set it up on the kitchen table. It didn't take her long to find a news article about the man's death — any sort of unexpected death was big news in Vista — but she had to do some digging to find out more than the newswoman on television had told her.

Eventually, she found a short post on a social media website from a local hiking group the man had been part of, which gave her his name. Gunnar Williams. She committed it to memory, then, hoping against hope that his cause of death had nothing to do with his fall in the cookie shop, she continued to search for clues to how he had died. Frustratingly, she found nothing. *Maybe they'll update it soon*, she thought. She bit her lip, then shut the laptop. It would eat at her until she knew the truth, but refreshing the same page over and over again wouldn't do her any good.

Lilah managed to eat breakfast, even though her anxiety made the oatmeal bland and tasteless, then finished her morning routine. By the time she sat down in front of the computer again, an hour had passed. It wasn't much time, but she couldn't wait any longer. She had to know how the man had died. It took her a while, but eventually she found a comment nestled in the same post where she had found his name.

*I'm so sorry. What happened?*

*He suffered a traumatic head injury. We aren't sure exactly what happened, but the police think he was wandering around for at least an hour before he passed away. We're asking anyone with information about what happened to step forward.*

At the end of the comment was the same number that Lilah had seen on the television earlier. Feeling numb with shock, she slowly shut the computer. Her whole body felt cold. She realized that she was

KILLER VALENTINE COOKIES BOOK FIVE IN KILLER COOKIE COZY MYSTERIES

shaking. This couldn't be real. It just couldn't. Was she dreaming? She pinched herself, but the pain did nothing to snap her out of it.

*He died because of me*, she thought. *I killed him. I didn't mean to, of course, but does that really matter?* A man was dead, and she had to face the fact that she was responsible, not only for his death, but for the loss of the cookie shop. Surely it wouldn't survive this. Once she came clean about what had happened, The Casual Cookie would be shut down.

She knew that she would call that number at the bottom of the screen, but not yet. First, she wanted to take one last look at what she had built. The cookie shop was the only good thing she had ever done with her life, and she couldn't bear the thought of never again opening the doors to the public.

"I'll call tonight," she promised herself. "After I get home from work, I'll tell the truth about what happened, and face whatever consequences there are." She owed that to the man who had lost his life because of her lack of responsibility. She would do the right thing… just not right away.

# CHAPTER FOUR

Her misery seemed to shield her from the rain as she walked to work. She got wet, but she hardly noticed the soaking. She wanted to cry, but the tears wouldn't come — or maybe they did, but the rain washed them away.

After entering the dry, warm cookie shop, she stripped off her outer layer of clothing and grabbed a fresh sweater from her bag. Even with her waterproof windbreaker and an umbrella, the water had found its way into every nook and cranny. Even after getting into dry clothes, she still felt damp, and hoped her hair would dry sufficiently while she baked.

It felt good to dive back into the normal routine of taking stock of the inventory, pulling out the ingredients and lining them up neatly on the counter, and turning the radio on to her favorite station. With her hands washed, her sleeves pushed up, and an apron tied on, she dove into the first batch of cookies that she had to make that morning.

Although The Casual Cookie had a variety of premium cookies, the favorites were the classics. Lilah sold many more double chocolate chunk cookies, iced sugar cookies, and pumpernickel cookies than she did s'mores cookies, pumpkin spice cookies, or cookies filled with a gooey center. She was surprised at the number of cookies that she went through, and had learned to make more than she thought she'd need so that she wouldn't have to run back into the kitchen to make more in the middle of the day.

As she worked now, she thought back on the bittersweet memories of her first months running the cookie shop. To say there had been a learning curve would be an understatement, but she had persevered, and had ended up coming out on top. Now, all of that would have been for nothing and she would spend the rest of her life bearing the guilt of knowing someone had died because of her, no matter how accidentally.

The tears finally came as she was stirring together the ingredients for a batch of chocolate chunk cookies. She put the spoon down and sat on a stool, hiding her face in her hands as she sobbed. She found herself wishing that she could turn back time to fix what she had done. How could one tiny mistake change so much?

After a little while, she took a shuddering breath, straightened up, and walked over to the sink to wash her hands and splash cold water on her face. She had given herself one last day to say goodbye to the cookie shop, and she had better get to it. The cookies wouldn't bake themselves, after all. She wanted today to be perfect.

It was still pelting rain by the time she switched on the open sign and unlocked the doors. The rain, she knew, would slow business down, but she usually got a nice trickle of customers even on the worst days. With luck, it would stop raining by the time people began getting off of work, and things would pick up toward the evening. Lilah sat behind the register, feeling sentimental as she looked around the little shop. She knew every inch of the place, and it had come to feel like a second home. Feeling tears prick her eyes again, she blinked rapidly. She wanted to enjoy today, not cry the whole time. There would be plenty of time for that later.

The door opened, and in walked her first customer of the day. She straightened up and smiled. The expression froze on her face as she realized who was walking in. Margie. She had been too embarrassed to see her neighbor the night before, but somehow the whole mess with the car didn't seem as important now that someone had died.

"There you are," her neighbor said as she shook her umbrella off. "I was beginning to think that you had vanished from the face of the earth. I figured my best chance to find you was to catch you here."

"Sorry, I've been… well, I've had a lot going on. How have you been?"

"Well, I'm hoping this cold snap ends soon, but overall I've been well. I got some good news that I wanted to share with you. I stopped by your house last night, but you must have been out. I thought you might have found a way to go see your father, so I didn't call you… but the insurance came through. I'll be picking up a new car sometime this week, so everything is fine. You'll have your car back, and I'll get a new one."

"Oh, Margie, that's wonderful," Lilah said, feeling the lump return to her throat. "I'm so sorry. I can't say it enough. If there's anything I can do, let me know. If your insurance premium goes up, I'll help pay it, or —"

"Nonsense. It could have happened to me just as easily as it did to you. I think most people would have swerved if a dog ran into the road. I'm just glad *you* didn't get hurt. Cars are replaceable, but people aren't. Besides, you've been letting me use your car, even though I told you I'd manage just fine without one. Don't tell me you walked to work today in this?" Margie gestured through the front window, where the rain was still coming down.

"I brought a change of clothes," Lilah said. "I didn't have any other options, and I didn't want to bother anyone else."

"You should have called me," the older woman said, shaking her head. "If I didn't know better, I'd think you were avoiding me. I'll pick you up this evening, so you don't have to get drenched on your way back."

"I'm hoping the rain will stop. And you don't have to do that, Margie. You do too much for me."

"Well, if you want to do something for me in return, you can come with me to pick up my new car in a couple of days. That way you can drive yours home, and I won't have to worry about it."

"Of course," she said. "I don't know what I'd do without you." To her horror, she began crying again.

"Lilah, what's wrong?" her neighbor asked, her voice full of concern. Unable to keep it in any longer, Lilah told her everything.

"There, there," the older woman said a few minutes later. She patted her on the back, and passed her a handful of napkins. "Whatever happened, it wasn't your fault. I think you should make that call right now, and get all of this off of your chest. Won't you feel better when you know what's going to happen?"

"I'm going to lose everything," Lilah sniffed. "And I feel terrible for even thinking about that, considering that poor man is dead, but I can't stop wondering how I'm going to survive. All of my money is tied up in this shop — and a lot of your money too. I'll have to start working at the diner again, if Randall will take me back, but I could barely make ends meet when I worked there before. I don't think it will be enough with the debt I have now."

"You don't know that you're going to lose anything," the older woman said. "Don't drive yourself crazy thinking about what might happen."

"You really think I should call now?"

Margie nodded. "Honesty is the best policy. Putting it off won't help anyone."

"Okay." She took a deep breath. "Will you wait here while I call?"

"Of course. Just take a moment to get yourself under control, then go on back into the kitchen. I'll handle things out here."

Lilah found the number easily enough. News of the man's death seemed to be everywhere she looked online. Every time she saw mention of his name, or his family, she felt a surge of guilt. Her stomach was in knots as she dialed, but she knew that Margie was right. It was better to call now. She should have called as soon as she had heard about his death that morning.

# CHAPTER FIVE

S he walked out of the kitchen a few minutes later, still in shock. After dropping her phone on the counter, she turned slowly to face her friend. Margie was looking at her expectantly, her face full of sympathy.

"I didn't do it," Lilah said.

"You didn't make the call?"

"No, I did. I didn't kill him."

"What did they say?"

Lilah took a deep breath. "I told them about his fall here at The Casual Cookie, and that he bumped the back of his head on the counter. I told the woman that I'd come into the police station right away if she needed me to. I feel bad for her — I was a mess. She told me that he was found with a serious injury to the temple, not to the back of his head, and that it was bleeding and not at all as minor as I had described. I answered a few more questions for her and gave her my number, and that was it. There's no way that his injury was from what happened here."

"Oh, Lilah, I'm so glad. What about the woman he was with?"

"Me too." A broad grin spread across her face. Of course, she was still concerned about her father, but at least he was on the road to recovery. Her livelihood was safe. "The woman was his fiancée. They had already spoken to her. They didn't tell me much, about that, though. You have no idea how much better I feel. I'm sorry for crying so much earlier. You must think I'm crazy."

"Not at all. You had every reason to think what you did. Any normal person would have felt the way."

"Thank you so much for coming here today, Margie. If you hadn't shown up and talked some sense into me, I would have spent all day a miserable wreck until I called this evening."

"That's what friends are for," the older woman said with a smile. "Now, how about a cookie? I didn't come in here *just* to see you, you know."

"Take whatever you like," Lilah said, laughing. "You know you're always free to help yourself."

"Won't you eat one with me? There is something else I wanted to talk about, besides the car."

"Okay. I've got time to sit for a bit. It's not busy at all, thanks to the rain."

The two of them settled into a little table in the corner by the wide front window. The rain was much more pleasant to look at now that Lilah knew she wouldn't be walking home through it. It would have been the perfect day to curl up in front of a fire with a book, which was probably what most of her customers were doing right now, instead of venturing out in search of a cookie. Lilah had a warm salted caramel cookie in front of her, and Margie had settled on a couple of small shortbread cookies. Lilah broke a piece off of hers and popped it into her mouth, enjoying the rich, full flavor. Everything seemed so much brighter now that she knew that she wasn't responsible for anyone's death.

"I want you to tell me what's going on between you and Reid," Margie said without preamble. "I thought everything was going well between the two of you?"

"It was," Lilah said. "Has he said anything?"

The other woman shook her head. "He stopped by the other day to take care of some branches that had fallen in my yard, and when I asked him how you were, he clammed right up. I could tell by the look in his eyes that something had happened, but I didn't press."

Lilah raised her eyebrows. She didn't quite believe *that*. Margie loved to involve herself in other people's lives. The year before, she had relentlessly tried to set her and Reid up. The fact that they had eventually started dating had a lot to do with the woman sitting across the table from her right now.

"I screwed it up, as usual," she said, sighing. "He told me he loved me. I didn't say anything. As in, I panicked, and clammed up for about five minutes until I asked him to pass the TV remote."

Margie gave a silent whistle. "I can see how that might have upset him. But you two are good now?"

"No, it gets worse," Lilah groaned. "He asked me about it a few days later, and I told him I didn't know how I felt. He pointed out that we've been dating for nearly a year, and if those feelings weren't there yet, then maybe they never would be. Somehow, we ended up arguing and I told him that we should put our relationship on hold. Then, of course, the whole thing with my dad and your car happened, and somehow two weeks have gone by without us talking once."

"Oh, Lilah. I'm so sorry. I'm sure the two of you will make up… if that's what you want."

"I miss him," she said. "But how do I know if I love him?"

"You just… know." Margie had a faraway look in her eyes, and Lilah guessed that she was thinking about her husband, who had died years ago. "He should be the person you feel like you can't live without. The one you want to share all of your special moments with and the one you want to tell everything to. Relationships start with a spark, but to last, there has to be an ember that never dies."

"All I know is that I miss him, and I want him to be happy," Lilah said with a sigh. "He's different than the other guys I've dated. It feels so much more serious, and I thought I wanted that, but it's also sort of frightening."

"Take your time," her friend suggested. "Figure out what you want, even if it isn't what he wants. You know I adore both of you, and I don't want either of you to be upset, but there's no sense in wasting time on a relationship that you know isn't going anywhere."

"I know. I guess I've got a lot of thinking to do. It can wait until later, though; right now, I just want to celebrate the fact that I didn't kill anyone. Who would have thought that being innocent would feel so good?"

It wasn't until after her friend left that Lilah began to wonder what had really happened to Gunnar Williams. It had been wonderful to discover that she was off the hook for his death, but *something* had still happened to him, and it had been something terrible by the sound of it. If she didn't kill him, then who did? Was there a murderer in the sleepy little town of Vista?

PATTI BENNING

# CHAPTER SIX

O ne of the benefits of being back on speaking terms with Margie was that Lilah felt comfortable enough to use her car when her friend didn't need it. Her spirits were still lifted the next day, and the weather didn't do anything to bring her down. The rain had stopped, though clouds still scuttled across the mottled blue sky, and the temperature had risen from the low forties to an almost balmy feeling sixty degrees. While most of the country was slogging through a few feet of snow, Lilah was able to go to the grocery store without wearing a coat in the middle of winter.

Lilah tried her best to ignore the pink and red Valentine's Day decorations that the grocery store had put up. She had a list, but the only things on it were cookie supplies. For her own personal groceries, she was much less organized. She had long had a habit of grabbing whatever looked good off of the shelves, and even though she kept meaning to make a meal plan each week, it never quite seemed to happen.

It was hard to imagine what a dark place she had been in the day before. Nothing had really changed, but knowing that the man's death hadn't been her fault made all the difference. *I'll grab this brownie mix to celebrate*, she thought. *Even I can't eat cookies all the time.* Despite her sadness at the thought of spending the coming holiday alone, she grabbed a package of red food coloring as well. She might not be in the holiday mood, but many of her customers certainly were.

She had just put a gallon of milk into her car, when from behind her she heard, "Lilah?" The voice was one she recognized immediately. She spun around to find Reid standing behind her, with his own cart in front of him.

"Hi," she said, too surprised to say anything more. He was the last person that she had expected to run into, and she felt completely unprepared.

"What are you doing here?" he asked. "Well, obviously you're shopping, but I guess I thought you'd be at work."

"I usually don't get there for another hour." She frowned. "Are you avoiding me?" The thought of him actively avoiding the places she might be bothered her.

He shifted, looking uncomfortable. "No. I just wasn't expecting to see you. That's all."

They stood in uncomfortable silence for a moment before Lilah cleared her throat. "Well, it was nice seeing you. I should finish shopping."

"Me too. I'll see you around."

He stepped forward and they gave each other an awkward hug. Lilah turned back to her cart and made it only a few steps away before she heard him speak again.

"Lilah — do you have to time grab a cup of coffee with me?"

She hesitated for a beat, then smiled. "Sure."

They met at Randall's diner, where she had worked on and off ever since she moved to Vista. Randall had been good to her, and even though she had a steady business of her own now, she still stopped in often. An added benefit was that it was close to her house, which made it easy for her to meet Reid there before she went to work, after dropping the groceries off at her house.

"So, what have you been up to?" Reid asked as the waitress filled up their coffee mugs. She wasn't anyone that Lilah knew, but part of her was glad the one of her friends hadn't been on shift today. Gossip spread quickly in the small town, and it was hard to keep anything a secret.

"Work, mostly," she said. "I've had some family stuff going on too."

"Is everyone alright?"

"My dad collapsed a couple of weeks ago. He ended up in the hospital, and they've been doing a lot of testing. They found something — a shadow — in his brain, and are going to go in for a biopsy soon."

"I'm sorry. That's got to be rough. He's a strong guy, though. I'm sure he'll pull through."

"I hope so. I've only seen him once, back when it first happened. It was weird seeing him lying in that hospital bed. He has always seemed invincible, and it's unsettling to see him looking so helpless."

"You should have called me. I would have gone with you. That's not the sort of thing anyone should go through alone."

"Yeah." She looked down at her slightly greasy coffee. Randall's had great food, but she couldn't say the same about its hot drinks. "It's okay. It was a family thing. Margie let me borrow her car since mine has been acting up again. Then I crashed it on the way back, but she probably told you about that."

"I knew her car got wrecked, but she didn't say how," he said, sounding surprised. "Are you all right?"

"I bumped my head, but other than a bruise, I was fine. It's mostly faded now, but it looked pretty nasty for a while. I felt terrible about the car, but I guess her insurance is paying for it."

"That's good. It sounds like you've had a lot to worry about."

"You don't know the half of it," she said with a faint smile, thinking about everything that had happened the day before. "How have you been?"

"I've been okay. Working, spending some time with my niece and nephew, nothing out of the ordinary. The kids hate being back at school after the holiday."

"I bet they do," she said, smiling. "How are they doing? I miss seeing them."

"Besides the complaints about school, they're doing pretty well," he said with a chuckle. "If I end up watching them again this weekend, we'll stop by the cookie shop."

"Good," she said. "It will be nice to have the three of you visit."

They fell silent, until Reid spoke a few moments later. "Lilah… I'm sorry. I didn't mean to pressure you about anything. I've been trying to give you space, but it sucks. I miss you."

Lilah's stomach did a flip. "I miss you too, Reid. Now isn't really the best time to talk about all of this. Yesterday was pretty much the worst day ever, and I'm still recovering. And I've got to get to work, or I won't have time to do everything I need to before opening. Can we do this later?"

He nodded. "Just let me know when is a good time. Like I said, I'll try to bring the kiddos in this weekend. I'll see you then. Thanks for grabbing coffee with me."

She gave him a small smile as she stood up. "It was nice to see you. Have a good day, alright? We'll talk soon, I promise."

She dropped a couple of dollar bills by the register as she left. She had hoped Randall would come out so she could see him, but she would have to say hi another time. She really was cutting it close; the cookie shop was supposed to open soon, and she still had a couple of batches of cookies to get in the oven. Seeing Reid again had been worth it, though. Despite her uncertainty over the future of their relationship, she *had* missed him, and it was good to know that he was doing well. She wasn't sure what she would say when they finally got together for the talk that they needed to have, but she had hopes that no matter what happened, they would be able to remain friends.

PATTI BENNING

# CHAPTER SEVEN

Two batches of heart shaped sugar cookies sat on the counter cooling while Lilah colored two bowls of icing; one pale pink and the other red. While she worked, she had been thinking about what exactly it was that she enjoyed about her job so much, and had concluded that it had everything to do with creativity. Every single day she had the opportunity to create something new, and she was completely free to utilize any idea that she came up with.

Today was dedicated to frosting cookies instead of coming up with new recipes, and she enjoyed seeing the growing pile of hearts on the counter. She had even bought a few small canisters of edible glitter, which she used to add pizazz to some of the cookies. She knew it seemed a bit silly to spend so much time on cookies that would just end up being eaten, but presentation went a long way in the cookie selling business. Besides, she enjoyed it, so why not do it?

As she worked, she found herself thinking once more about Gunnar Williams. *How* had he died? Had someone attacked him? She remembered what he had said after his fall, about how he didn't need the money he would get from suing her, and she seemed to remember him saying something about that day being an especially good one. Had he recently come into a lot of money? Could that have had something to do with his death? Surely he hadn't been carrying the money around with him?

*Maybe he was involved in something bad,* she thought. She didn't like to think bad things about the dead, but it was a question that was begging to be asked. While it was possible that he had fallen a second time and sustained a more serious head injury than the one he had gotten at the cookie shop, she thought that much of a coincidence was unlikely. Someone must have attacked him, and money seemed like it would have been a good motivation. *I should have told the police about what he said when I called yesterday,* she thought. *I was so upset I didn't even think about it.*

She took a fresh batch of cookies off of the cooling rack and began to ice them, her hands working automatically as she lost herself in thought. It had been a long time since something like this had happened in Vista. Even though she knew she hadn't had anything to do with the man's death, she still felt connected to him somehow. She had very likely been one of the last people to see him alive. She wanted to find out what had happened to him for her own peace of mind, and also for the safety of everyone else in town.

She was halfway through icing the last cookie when she heard the bell out front ring. Today hadn't been as slow as yesterday had been, but she had had enough time between customers to get some work done in the back. She had been toying with the idea of hiring an employee for a while, but she didn't think it was worth it, at least not yet. It would complicate everything from taxes to her insurance, and would be a cut into the profits that she didn't think was justifiable until things began to get busier. That meant that for now, she was stuck juggling customers and baking. If one person decided to buy the entire stock of a certain type of cookie, it threw her whole day out of whack, but most of the time it worked out okay.

"Hi, welcome to The Casual Cookie," she said, dusting flour off of her apron as she came out front. "What can I get for you?"

"Are you the store owner?" the woman asked.

Lilah nodded. "I'm Lilah Fallon. Owner, and for the time being, the only person who works here."

"Great, you're who I need to talk to, then," the woman said, giving her a wan smile. "You do bulk orders of cookies, right?"

"Occasionally," Lilah said, perking up. "What are you looking for?"

"I'm planning my brother's wake, and trying to find places that will cater with such short notice is tough," the woman said. "So, I guess I'll take whatever you can do."

"I'm sorry for your loss. Did you want a specific kind of cookie? Do you know his favorite type?"

"I'm not sure. Could you just do a variety? I think I'll need about a hundred. The wake is next Wednesday."

"I can do that. Here, let me take down your information."

She rummaged around for a pen and a pad of paper, and passed it over to the woman, asking her to fill out her name and telephone number. When she took it back, she raised her eyebrows in surprise. "Your last name is Williams? Your brother wasn't Gunnar Williams, by any chance?"

The woman, Rosella, nodded. "Yes, that's him. Did you hear about what happened on the news, or did you know him personally?"

"He stopped in my store the day he died," Lilah said. "I can't imagine what you're going through. It must be hard."

"Hard doesn't even begin to cover it," Rosella said. "Thank you for this. I know it's super last minute and right before Valentine's Day. His fiancée offered to help, but she's a mess, and besides, they hadn't been together for very long. He's family, and I need to do this myself."

"It's no problem," Lilah promised. "If you need me to work with you on the price, I can."

"I just want everything to be nice for him," the other woman said. "Money isn't an issue. Call me if you need any more information. Otherwise, I'll pick the cookies up Wednesday morning."

After Rosella left, Lilah returned to the kitchen to continue icing the cookies. She would have been excited to get a bulk order, but the fact that it was for a wake dampened her happiness. The fact that it was for Gunnar's wake made it even worse, somehow. What were the chances that his sister would have chosen to come to the cookie shop? *It isn't that big of a coincidence,* she told herself. It wasn't as if there were very many catering options in Vista, and as Rosella had said, most places were already booked in advance.

The past few days had given her a lot to think about. She didn't think she had ever experienced so many ups and downs in her life. At least her relationship with Margie was mended, and it seemed as though she and Reid might be able to work things out as well. She wasn't going to lose the cookie shop, and no matter how Gunnar Williams had died, it hadn't been her fault. That had to count for something,

# CHAPTER EIGHT

"Perfect." Lilah touched her phone's screen and it made a digital clicking sound, capturing the image of the Valentine's Day cookies arranged on a plate. She sent the photo to her mother's cell phone number, along with the text, *I'll try to visit soon and when I do I'll bring some for you and Dad!*

It was evening, and she had been home for a couple of hours already. She had brought a box of cookies home with her, and had already eaten far too many. Arranging the plate to take over to Margie's had been a spur of the moment idea, and she was glad that she had thought of it. Her neighbor would want to hear all about her coffee date with Reid, and Lilah wanted her advice on what to do next.

The older woman filled an odd void in her life; she acted almost like a surrogate parent to Lilah, who had never had that great a relationship with her own parents, and she had also become a close friend. Margie had children of her own — and grandchildren, too — but none of her family lived in town. The two of them might have seemed like an odd pair, but Lilah didn't know where she would be without Margie's friendship. She knew that she certainly wouldn't have had the cookie shop, and she probably wouldn't have ever dated Reid either.

"I'll be right back, you two," Lilah said to her pets as she pulled on her shoes. "Don't get into anything while I'm gone. I'll clean the kitchen when I get back."

She grabbed the platter of cookies and headed out the front door and across the yard to her neighbor's house. Margie opened her door just moments after Lilah knocked on it.

"Those look lovely," she said as Lilah entered her kitchen.

"They're all for you. I brought too many home. I spent a lot of time icing them today, and it would be a shame to see them go to waste."

"Let me pour a glass of milk, then I'll try one. Do you want to sit down for a bit? Would you like something to drink, too?"

"I'll just have a glass of water," Lilah said. "I'll sit for a little while, but I left some dinner dishes out that I should take care of soon."

The two of them sat and talked for the next twenty minutes. Lilah enjoyed just relaxing with her friend. It had been too long since they had done this, though she knew that was all on her.

"When do you pick up your new vehicle?" she asked.

"Wednesday morning," Margie said. "Will you be able to go with me?"

"That should work. I'll just have to make sure I finish the cookies the night before. Someone ordered a hundred of them for a wake on Wednesday."

She realized that she hadn't told her friend about Gunnar's sister coming into the shop. She launched into the story, and when she was finished, she asked, "What do you think? Is it weird that she stopped there?"

"Weird? I don't think so. You are the only cookie shop in town, and most places book at least a couple of weeks in advance anyway. Why, do you think it's odd?"

"Maybe slightly. I mean, The Casual Cookie is one of the last places her brother ever went. But I think you're probably right. It's just a coincidence."

"I feel bad for her. I'm glad that you're able to help her out. Besides, it will be good practice. You haven't had many catering opportunities."

"I've had a few smaller ones," she said. "I've got a couple of birthday parties. It's just hard to get my name out there. I need to start advertising in some of the other nearby cities. Of course, if I get too busy, I'll have to think about hiring someone else to work for me, and that will be a huge rabbit hole I'm not sure I want to go down yet."

"I'm impressed at how well you've been doing everything on your own," her friend said. "I know the cookie shop keeps you busy, but you've done a great job."

"Thank you. That –" Her phone rang, cutting her off. She looked at the caller ID. It was her mother, who probably wanted to see when she was planning on visiting. She muted the call, then looked up at Margie. "I should call her back. I had better head home. I'll make sure I remember about Wednesday, and I'm sure I'll see you before then."

"Thanks for the cookies," Margie said. "I appreciate them."

Lilah walked back over to her house and kicked off her shoes as she walked into the living room. Her mother had left a voicemail, but she didn't bother to listen to it. She hit the button to call the woman back.

"Hi, Mom. What's going on? Is Dad alright?"

"That's what I was calling you about," her mother said. "The doctors gave him the okay to come home.

He's on some medications, but they think he will be fine."

"That's wonderful," she said. "What about the shadow they saw on his brain?"

"It's smaller now. They think he had a mini stroke, and the shadow was from bleeding in his brain. It's scary, but they said he got lucky. He is supposed to rest for the next couple of weeks, but you know how he is. It's going to be tough to keep him from going into work."

"I'm so glad that they are releasing him. I will try to visit you guys soon. I might be able to come up the weekend after Valentine's Day."

"Why don't you spend the whole weekend with us?"

"You know I can't. I have the animals, and the cookie shop to run," Lilah said.

"This whole thing with your father has made me think about how short life is. You should try to visit more, at least."

"I'll try," she promised. "Either way, I'll see you guys sometime soon. Call me when he gets settled in, so I can talk to him."

"I will. I hope everything is going well for you."

"The Casual Cookie is doing wonderfully," she said. "Time seems to have flown. I can't believe it's been open for a whole year already."

"Just don't get your hopes up too high yet. Your father said that most small businesses fail within the first five years. If you make it past that, you should be good to go."

"Thanks, Mom," she said dryly. "I love the vote of confidence."

"I just want you to be realistic," her mother said. "I hope you have a backup plan in case it fails. You know your father and I both worry about you."

"I know," she said. "Thanks for calling me about Dad. I'm glad that he's doing better, and I'll try to come up next weekend. I've got to go now."

"Okay. I'll talk to you sometime tomorrow when your father gets home."

Lilah hung up, feeling frustrated. Even after a year, her parents still tended to treat the cookie shop like another one of her crazy ideas. She knew that it would take them some time to realize that this was actually what she was going to do with her life. She was glad that her father was able to leave the hospital, at least. Even though her relationship with her parents was tense, she still loved them.

A knock sounded at her front door. Thinking that it was Margie, she got up and answered it without looking out the window first. She was surprised to see a man that she didn't recognize, dressed in some sort of brown uniform with a ball cap pulled low over his face.

"Can I help you?" she asked, pushing Winnie back with one foot as the dog tried to greet the visitor.

"Ms. Fallon?" the man said.

"Yes," she said. "That's me."

"I have a package for you. Fill out your information here."

He pushed a pad of paper toward her, and she scribbled her name and birthdate. Her eyes were glued to a square package the size of the microwave sitting on the stoop next to him.

"Who is it from?" she asked.

"No idea," he said. "There's no return address. Thanks." He tipped his hat even further down on his head and spun on his heel, walking down the pathway.

Bursting with curiosity, Lilah grabbed the package and took it inside. She set it on the kitchen counter and grabbed a knife from the knife block to cut the tape. As she did so, her eyes caught sight of the clock on the stove. It was almost nine. She frowned, hesitating. What delivery service delivered packages so late? Why hadn't she seen any identification symbols on the man's uniform?

She stared at the package, torn. Something about the delivery felt off, but she couldn't figure out why. The delivery driver had probably just been late on his rounds. After all of the business with Gunnar's death, she was probably just being paranoid.

She sliced through the tape and pulled the box open. Buried in the packing peanuts were a couple of smaller packages. One held a variety of fun cookie cutters, including one shaped like a beagle, and the other was packed with cookie decorating supplies, one of which was a packet of shiny edible beads that she had been searching for in stores for quite a while.

Lilah emptied out the box and searched everywhere for a name or some indication of whom it had come from, but she couldn't find anything. Confused and still somewhat unsettled, she set the box back on the counter and begin cleaning up the packing peanuts. She wasn't sure what to make of this gift. Whoever had gone through the trouble of buying it for her knew her quite well, but it was someone that she knew, why wouldn't they have left their name?

# CHAPTER NINE

S he worked through the weekend, wondering about the package on and off, but finding no answers. The cookie cutters came in handy, and she had fun making different shapes of sugar cookies and decorating them. When Reid stopped in on Saturday with his niece and nephew, she spent nearly an hour visiting with them in the store, and letting them try all sorts of different cookies. The two of them didn't get the chance to talk, at least not about any adult matters, but it was nice to see him again. She was still torn about how she wanted to handle their upcoming discussion. Did she love him? Was Margie right, and if she did, would she just know?

She was at the age where her biological clock was ticking. If she wanted to get married and have kids, she would have to do it sooner rather than later. While she liked children, having her own had never been at the top of her priority list. She felt like she was hardly responsible to take care of herself, let alone another human being. As far as marriage went, well it was something that she definitely wanted, but she had always thought it would happen in the future -- sometime far away, when she had her life more together.

If Reid wanted a more serious relationship, instead of just casually dating like she was used to, then she knew that the discussion of marriage and kids would be on the table soon enough after they talked about love. They had been seeing each other for nearly a year, and had known each other for longer. Was she ready for all that? No matter how many times she asked herself that question, no answer came to her.

"Thanks, Lilah, we had fun," his niece, Alisha, said as she and her brother left the store. "I love your cookies. They're always so pretty, and they taste amazing too."

"Thanks, Alisha," she said. "You know that you and your brother are welcome here anytime."

"Don't tell them that. They'll come in every day after school, and then my sister would kill me," Reid said. "Now, if you had a salad shop, she might appreciate it."

Lilah laughed. "If I owned a salad shop, I would probably be out of business by now. I'm glad you guys stopped in. It was nice to see everybody."

"When do you want to get together again?" he asked.

"Well," she paused, thinking, "I was going to finally take down my Christmas tree on Monday. Margie told me about this person who takes old Christmas trees and feeds them to her goats, so I was going to donate it. Do you want to come with me? I could use some help, I suppose."

"I'll see if I can get the time off work," he said. "The factory is shutting down on Thursday while some new machines are installed, so the first part of that week might be a little bit busy, but I should be able to manage it."

"Great," she said, giving him a smile. She barely stopped herself before she said, "it's a date."

With her father out of the hospital now, the only thing she had left to worry about was Reid. She spent all day Sunday thinking about him, and their possible future together, and Monday morning she woke up with butterflies in her stomach. She was looking forward to seeing him, but she was not looking forward to the talk that she knew they would have.

Reid met Lilah at her house. She had already taken all of the decorations off of the tree, but hadn't been able to get it out of the stand on her own. The bowl was still filled with water, so she couldn't tip it on its side to make things easier for herself.

"I should have brought my leather gloves," he said as they arranged themselves on either side of the tree, both of them gingerly reaching for the trunk through the prickly needles.

"Sorry," she said. "I have some gardening gloves, but they aren't much help. Are you ready?"

"Ready."

They lifted together, and the tree came out. Lilah began to walk backward, trying not to knock over anything important, and didn't put the tree down until they reached the kitchen, where they paused just long enough for her to open the kitchen door.

With a feeling of relief, she helped Reid toss the tree out into the front yard.

"We made quite the mess," he said, sounding amused.

Lilah turned to see a trail of fallen pine needles through her house. "Oh," she said in a small voice. "Wow."

"I'll help you clean up," he said with a chuckle. "Then we can go and deliver this thing to the goats."

Delivering the tree was easier said than done. Reid eyed Lilah's little car doubtfully, then offered to use his own.

"I couldn't let you do that," she said. "It might scratch the top of your car, and besides, the needles will get everywhere."

"The tree is longer than your car, and probably heavier than it."

"It is not," she said. "My car will be fine. We just have to tie it down securely; I don't want it falling off in the middle of the road."

"If you insist," he said. "I don't know if your poor car will ever forgive you for this."

She made a face at him, then they both laughed. It was nice, just spending time with him again. She was still smiling even after they wrestled the tree on top of the car and she had sustained a few more scratches from the needles, and wondered what she had been thinking when she had let their relationship fall apart.

"Do you want me to drive?" he asked.

"I can do it," she said. "You just keep an eye on the tree. Turn the side mirror up so you can see it and let me know if it moves."

They rode in silence for the first few minutes, then Reid struck up a conversation. "So, how are you?"

"I'm fine," she said. Realizing that her answer might come across as her being shorter with him than she intended to be, she added, "The cookie shop is doing well. I've got some extras at home if you want to take them with you later."

"Are you still making too many every day?"

"I'd rather have too many than not enough," she said. "At least the extra ones don't go to waste. A diet of cookies probably isn't the healthiest thing, but I would feel bad just throwing them away."

Over the past year, she had managed to streamline the cookie making process quite a bit. Most of the cookie dough could be frozen for weeks, so she just had to remember to take out the frozen dough the night before so it could thaw before she made the cookies that she would need for the next day. She sold the fresh-baked cookies at full price, and day-old cookies at half-price. Anything that had been there for three days, she took home and gave to her friends or ate herself. The key for her was to make cookies in small batches, but to keep enough dough in the fridge that she could quickly make more if she ran out.

Of course, cooking the one hundred cookies for Rosella Williams on Wednesday would make her run out of a couple of things, and she would need to spend Thursday morning replenishing the supply of cookie dough.

They made it to the goat farm without incident, and she and Reid dropped off the tree. It had been a lot of work just to leave the tree for goats to eat, but she would have felt bad sending the tree to the dump. It had served her well over the holiday season, and at least now it would continue to make others happy… even if the others had four hooves and horns.

"Well, your car made it," he said when they got back. "I'm impressed."

"It may not look like much, but it's a tough little vehicle," she said.

He grinned at her, then his expression changed. He looked almost hesitant. "Look, I know that things haven't been right between us lately, but I've missed this. Do you want to go to the Valentine's Day parade with me on Tuesday evening? Just as friends, if that's what you want, but my niece and nephew will be there, and there will be food and candy. It might be nice."

"I'd like that," she said. "And Reid, thank you for helping today. I don't know if I would have been able to get the tree on the car by myself."

KILLER VALENTINE COOKIES BOOK FIVE IN KILLER COOKIE COZY MYSTERIES

"Of course you would have," he said. "I think you could do anything you set your mind to."

She didn't know how to reply to that. In an effort to disguise how flustered she was, she went into the kitchen and brought out a tray of cookies.

"I see you're enjoying the new cookie cutters," he said, smiling as he picked up a beagle shaped sugar cookie.

"The cookie-cutters… was that package from you?" she asked. "The guy who delivered it had no idea who it was from. You should've left your name."

"I left that package on your doorstep," he said, frowning. "No one delivered it. I stopped by myself and dropped it off."

Lilah felt her stomach drop. "A man wearing a brown uniform stopped by to give it to me," she said. "I signed for it and everything."

Reid stared at her, his eyes concerned. "I have no idea what's going on," he said. "I swear, I put it on your stoop with my own two hands. Do you think we should call the police?"

"And tell them what? It's not like he stole the package. I don't think anything he did was a crime…"

"What did he want your signature for?" he wondered.

"I have no idea." Her good mood was gone; she felt frightened now. "I wonder if it has something to do with what happened to Gunnar."

And then, of course, she had to tell him all about Gunnar Williams and what had happened in the cookie shop. It was late by the time they were done talking. Neither of them could find a connection between the mysterious man who had tricked her into giving her signature and Gunnar's death, but it was the only other odd thing that had happened to Lilah recently. There had to be some sort of connection.

"Thanks again for helping today," she said when she was done. "I know things have been weird between us and we need to talk about it, but all of this has been too much. I'm freaked out now, and worried about being alone in my own house. Can we just watch television and drink hot chocolate or something?"

"Of course, if that's what you want," he said. "You go make the drinks, and I'll turn on the TV."

When she came back into the living room with two mugs of hot cocoa a few minutes later, the television was turned onto a news program. She was only half listening as she scrolled through the emails on her phone, but when she heard the last name Williams, she snapped to attention. "The foundation that puts on the annual Valentine's Day parade would like to thank a new donor this year; Rosella Williams. She recently came into a large inheritance and wanted to give back to the community that she grew up in."

Lilah felt a tingle of suspicion. That must have been what Gunnar was talking about in the cookie shop. He must have only recently found out about the inheritance. With him dead now, all of that money would go to his sister, wouldn't it? It seemed like the mystery around his death just kept getting deeper. Whatever was happening, she knew one thing; she didn't want to be involved in it.

# CHAPTER TEN

O n Tuesday morning, Lilah woke up early. She had a lot of work to do if she wanted to have a hundred cookies ready to go by tomorrow. Since she had committed tomorrow morning to helping Margie get a new car, she had to make the cookies today.

She spent the morning shopping, making sure she had all the ingredients for the cookies that she was going to make. Rosella had said that she wanted a variety, and Lilah was going to give her one. Her own suspicions about Gunnar's death aside, she wanted his wake to be nice. There were a lot of unanswered questions, and she kept reminding herself that it wasn't her job to answer them. Her job was to make cookies and serve everyone with a smile. It was the best that she could do to brighten an otherwise sad day for his family.

She was almost sad to spend the whole day shut up in the cookie shop. The weather was beautiful, with sunshine and a temperature in the mid-fifties. Since the children were all out of school now, there was a lot of foot traffic, and it seemed to her that the bell at the front of the store rang almost continuously. Her pre-made balls of cookie dough seemed to disappear at an alarming rate as she baked and baked. She made hazelnut and chocolate cream cookies, gooey caramel cookies, buckeye cookies, and one of her personal favorites; peppermint and dark chocolate cookies. One thing that was missing from the variety was the brightly frosted sugar cookies that she had been making for the past few days. A wake was no place for a bright pink Valentine's heart cookie.

PATTI BENNING

By the end of the day, she had four boxes filled with twenty-five cookies each, plus a couple of extras just in case some got broken. She laid them out carefully, knowing that Rosella would be there as soon as the cookie shop opened the next day to pick them up.

She had gotten done just in time. The parade started in just an hour, and she still had to close the cookie shop and go home and change.

*At least I no longer go home smelling like burgers,* she thought. *That's one thing that I definitely like about not working at the diner.* Back when she had worked for Randall, she would go home at the end of every day smelling like grease and fried food. She greatly preferred smelling like vanilla and chocolate, even if she had flour on her clothes.

Things between her and Reid were still undecided. She knew that they had to have their talk at some point, but her stomach seemed to get in twists whenever she thought of it. She didn't want to have it before the parade, in case it went badly. Tomorrow, she had to help Margie with the car, then work for the last half of the day. She had assumed that her and Reid's Valentine's plans were canceled, but now she wasn't so sure. Anything could happen at the parade that evening.

At home, she changed into her nicest pair of dark jeans, a red sweater with gold threads woven throughout, and a comfortable pair of boots. Even though her future with Reid was one giant question mark, it was still nice to dress up for an evening out. She put on a pair of gold earrings, pulled her hair back, and took the time to do her makeup.

"Are the two of you going to be all right here tonight? I'm sorry to leave you alone again," she asked Winnie and Oscar. "I thought of bringing you along, Winnie, but you've been slipping out of your collar lately, and I don't want to chance you running into the parade. We'll figure out something new after this weekend. I've just been so busy lately. I'm sorry the two of you have been falling by the wayside."

She stroked her cat, then bent down to scratch behind Winnie's ears, making a silent promise to herself to set aside more time for her pets. When the doorbell rang a moment later, she assumed that it would be Reid, and was surprised to see Margie when she opened it.

"Well, I came by to see if you wanted to go to the parade together, but it looks like you're planning on going out already. Do you have a date?" Her friend's eyes twinkled.

"I'm going with Reid, but I don't know if it's a date," she said. "We're just going together. I'm sorry. If you want to come along with us –"

"Oh, no, no," her friend said. "I'm so happy the two of you are speaking again. You enjoy the evening with him. Don't you feel bad about me. I'll be meeting up with a couple of ladies from the library anyway."

"Maybe we'll see you there," Lilah said. "It's a nice night for it, at least."

"It should be beautiful. I love the Valentine's Day parade. I used to go every year with my husband. I think of him every time I see it."

"I'm sorry," Lilah said. "It must be hard."

"Hard? No, it's wonderful. It helps me feel closer to him. I've accepted that he's gone, though of course the first couple of years were difficult. Now, I'm just thankful whenever I see something that reminds me of him. I treasure all of our memories together, and even though sometimes it makes me sad to think that we'll never have any more, I wouldn't trade them away for anything."

Lilah bid her friend goodbye with a lump in her throat. She wished that she could one day have the same sort of relationship that Margie had had with her husband with her own man.

She was just about to shut the door when she saw a pair of headlights pull into the driveway. It was Reid this time. He got out of the car and walked toward the door. He seemed surprised to see her waiting for him.

"Am I late?"

"No, you're right on time," she said. "Margie just stopped by. I was talking to her before you got here.

"That reminds me, I promised her I would stop by and look at her washing machine. It's been acting up. Anyway, are you ready to go?"

"Just as soon as I grab my purse."

Not long after that, they were on their way into town. It was busier than she had ever seen it before. Reid had to park a couple of blocks away from Main Street, and they walked through the dark together to where the parade was being held, not quite touching. Just weeks ago, she would have taken Reid's hand. It was odd to be so close, and yet so far apart.

"It's a nice night," he commented.

"Yes, it is," she agreed. "I'm so glad it's not raining. I can't wait to see everything. I hope they have hot chocolate or apple cider."

"I'm sure they will. Do you want to do anything after this?"

"I'm not sure. Let's see how long we end up staying."

Lilah found a vendor that was handing out apple cider, then the two of them found a perfect spot to stand on the sidewalk by Main Street. It seemed as if the whole town had turned out for the parade. Vista went all out for every holiday, and Valentine's Day was no exception. She recognized a couple of people that stopped into the cookie shop regularly, and a few people from her time the diner. She really did love the little town. It was tiny, but that wasn't always a bad thing. Everyone knew each other, and on a night like this, it felt like a real community.

"Hey, that's Rosella," she said, gesturing to a woman a few feet down the sidewalk from them. She was standing by herself, gazing out across the street with a warm drink in her hand. "I'm going to go say hi and let her know the cookies are ready."

"Okay," Reed said. "I'll save our spot."

She walked over to the woman and cleared her throat. Rosella turned and looked at her blankly, but seemed to recognize her after a second.

"Oh, you're Lilah from the cookie shop, right?"

"I sure am," she said. "I just wanted to let you know that I got your order done earlier today. Are you sure you don't want me to deliver the cookies?"

"That's wonderful to hear. And no, I can pick them up. I'll head right past the store on my way to the funeral home anyway."

"Okay. I'll make sure to get there early and have everything ready for you. I'm sorry again for what you're going through."

"Thank you," the woman said. "I miss him already. We were close as children, but haven't been as close in recent years. I regret not spending more time with him. His death would have been a blow at any time, but it's doubly sad now. We had just gotten an inheritance from my grandparents, and he was so excited. He had all these big plans for it -- he was going to travel, see the world and all that. Then this

114

happened, and he never got to live his dream. He always enjoyed beautiful things, which is why I donated a portion of the money to this parade in honor of them."

"I'm sure he would've appreciated it," Lilah said. "I've got to get back to my friend; I think the parade is about to start. Just let me know if you change your mind about me delivering, and I'll bring the cookies over as quickly as possible."

She hurried back to Reid, thinking, *I was wrong about her. She sounds like she misses her brother, and she even donated some of the money. Why would someone do that with money that they killed for?*

# CHAPTER ELEVEN

By the time the parade started, Lilah was getting chilly. She hadn't brought a jacket; her sweater was the only layer she had worn. She shifted from foot to foot, trying to warm herself up by moving.

"Are you okay?" Reid asked.

"I'm just a bit cold," she said. "I'm sure I'll forget all about it by when the parade starts."

"Do you want to borrow my jacket?" he asked.

"I'll be fine," she said. "I don't want you to be cold too."

"I won't be cold," he said. "Here."

He shrugged off his jacket and handed it over to her. She took it hesitantly, putting on over her sweater. It felt wonderful to put on the warm jacket, and she smiled up at him. It felt good to be spending time with him again.

She heard music coming from the end of the street and turned to look. The parade was beginning. She watched as the floats came slowly into view, rolling down the street with a pink glow. It was less formal than the Christmas parade was, and people had fun with it. A little girl ran up to her and gave her a heart-shaped lollipop before giggling and running away again.

"It's been a while since I've seen something like this," she said. "It really is beautiful."

"It must take forever to organize," Reed said. "But I agree. It's beautiful."

They both fell silent as they continued to watch the parade. Lilah felt comfortable and happy. It would have been perfect if she hadn't still had Gunnar's death on her mind. That, plus the mysterious man who had delivered the package and had gotten her signature. Who *was* he? It didn't make sense at all. Why would anyone want her signature for something? Even more importantly, why would someone think that they had to trick her into signing something?

The parade passed by them gradually, then all at once it was over. Just because the floats were done, didn't mean that the town was done celebrating, and the townspeople began to mill about, chatting. Some of the stores were open late with special discounts, and there were food and drink vendors lining the sidewalk.

She and Reid decided to wander around and look at the stores for a little while before heading back to her house. If she hadn't gone on this outing with him, she may have kept the cookie shop open late, but she was glad that she had decided to go out instead. It felt good to be doing something outside of work.

They found Margie with her group of friends from the library at a dance studio that was giving away free gift bags. Lilah was glad to see that she was with friends, but she didn't stay to talk to her long. She was getting tired of walking around; she had been on her feet all day, baking cookies and serving her customers.

"Let's head back," she said to Reid after a little bit. He agreed, and they started the journey back to the car.

They were just about to turn off of Main Street when Lilah stopped mid-stride. She saw a man with a familiar brown hat walking through the crowd.

"Reid, it's him," she said. She grabbed his arm. He turned and looked, but the man was already gone. "Who?"

"The man who got my signature. I just saw him. I want to find out what he was doing at my house."

He followed her gaze, looking doubtful. She grabbed his hand reflexively and hurried forward, pushing through the crowd. At last, she caught sight of the man again. He wasn't in his uniform, but she recognized that brown hat and his closely trimmed hair. She hurried forward and reached for his arm, grabbing him by the sleeve. He turned around, shock on his face. He looked slightly familiar, beyond when she had seen him at her house, but she didn't know where else she might have run into him.

"Excuse me," she said, her voice sharp. "You're the one who delivered that package to me, aren't you?"

He looked from her to Reid, worried. "I don't know what you're talking about."

"You brought the box to my door and asked for my signature. I recognize your hat, and your hair…" She trailed off, because she recognized the man from somewhere else too. "You were in the cookie shop earlier this week."

She realized that was where she had seen him before. He had been the third person in the cookie shop the day that Gunnar Williams had been killed.

"So? I don't know why you're freaking out. It's a free country."

"I just want to know why you pretended to deliver a package to get my signature," she said.

"This is crazy, I've got to go. I don't have time for this."

He backed away, pulling out of her grip and first jogging, then running down the sidewalk through the crowd of people. Without thinking about it, Lilah took off after him. She heard Reid swear quietly behind her.

"Wait," she called. "I just wanted to talk to you."

He was forced to slow down when he nearly ran into a woman with a stroller. Lilah slipped past a young couple holding hands and grabbed onto his jacket again, forcing him to look at her.

"Tell me what is going on," she demanded.

"Look, I didn't mean anything bad by it," he said. "I needed a signature because I forged a request under your business license. I just needed to buy some stuff that you can only get with a valid business license. You seem so hassled and disorganized in the store, I thought you would be an easy mark. I didn't realize you were a crazy lady that would chase me through the street."

Lilah frowned at him. "What were you buying?"

He hesitated. "Energy drinks."

"What?" She let go of his jacket and stared at him, puzzled and not sure if she had heard him right.

"A buddy of mine and I got the idea to start selling these drinks... they're about four bucks in stores, and only a dollar each if you buy them wholesale, but you need a business license to buy them wholesale. I got your business license number from the framed license on the wall in the cookie store, but still needed your signature. I was going to make up some story about doing a survey for the city, but then

I saw the package in front of your house and decided to roll with it."

Lilah didn't know what to think. It was an unusual story, but she didn't have any reason not to believe him. Buying drinks wholesale from a distributor and then selling them on the side might be technically illegal, since he didn't have a permit to sell them, but it wasn't something malicious, as she had feared.

While she absorbed what he had said, he began to edge away again. "I'm sorry, alright? Can I go now?"

Before she could say anything else, he slipped away again. She didn't go after him this time.

"What was that all about?" Reid asked, looking miffed.

"That guy who got my signature," she said. "He said he needed to order energy drinks wholesale with a business license, and used my license number and signature to do it."

"I have no idea how you keep getting yourself into these messes," he said. "Do you want to go after him again?"

"No. I don't see what we would be able to do. Let's just go home. I don't know whether I believe him or not, but I can't do anything more about it now."

"All right," he said. "This has been an exciting evening. You lead an interesting life."

"I made a fool of myself, didn't I?" she asked, looking around. She had just chased a man and down Main Street at its busiest.

"I don't think too many people noticed," he said, putting an arm around her shoulders. "Even if they did, so what? Isn't there some sort of saying… there's no such thing as bad publicity?"

"I don't want people coming to The Casual Cookie just to laugh at me," she said. "I'm not that hard up for business."

He laughed, and they headed down the sidewalk together. Lilah looked over her shoulder, but the man was long gone by now.

# CHAPTER TWELVE

Even though she wasn't the one getting the new car, it was still fun to go with Margie to the auto lot the next morning while she picked up her vehicle. It made Lilah look at her little beat up vehicle in a whole new light. Maybe next year she would save up and get a nicer used car herself.

"This will take some getting used to," her friend said as she sat behind the wheel of her new car. "You'll have to show me how everything works. I've never had a car with a built-in GPS before. Of course, I hardly need it. I don't go that many new places. I suppose it will help when I go to visit my grandchildren this weekend."

"It's nice," Lilah said, sitting in the passenger seat and breathing in the new car smell. "I wish I didn't have to drive back in my falling apart little car."

"I'll give you a ride around town later this evening," her friend said. "We can test out all of the new features then. Thanks for coming with me. I know you have that order of cookies to worry about. A wake on Valentine's Day, though? That doesn't seem right."

"I got them done yesterday," Lilah said. "They're all packed up and ready to go. And Rosella said it was the first day they were available. She didn't realize it was on Valentine's Day until later, and by then it was too late to change it."

"Well, it can't be helped. You can't imagine how proud I am of you, Lilah. This cookie shop has been so good for you."

"It feels good to look back on all that I've accomplished," she said. "Well, I had better get going. I need to get to the cookie shop soon in case Rosella gets there early. I'll see you this evening, though."

She got out of the car and waved goodbye to her friend, then got into her own vehicle and drove toward The Casual Cookie. She was glad that Margie had finally gotten a replacement for the vehicle that she had wrecked. Her friend deserved something nice, and that car certainly was nice.

Her phone rang just before she got to the cookie shop. The number wasn't on her caller ID list, but it was local, so she answered it. It was Rosella Williams.

"I know I said I would pick up the cookies, but is there any way you can deliver them? It's been a terrible morning, and I'm running late."

"Just give me the address, and I'll get there soon as possible," Lilah said. She looked at the clock as she hung up. She would be cutting it close. She had to open the cookie shop soon, and she didn't want to be late for that. If she just drove there, dropped them off, and then went straight back to The Casual Cookie, she should have time.

It didn't take her long to grab the boxes of cookies and be on her way to the funeral home. She parked outside and looked around to see if there was anyone who could help her bring them in, but there wasn't. She stacked the boxes in her arms, balancing her chin on the top box as she walked inside.

A funeral home worker greeted her inside and directed her to the correct area. The room had already been set up, with photos of Gunnar everywhere. Lilah looked around, not sure where to put the cookies. There were a couple of long tables against one wall, though they didn't have any food on them yet, she guessed it was where the refreshments would go. She sat the boxes down, and was about to leave when she heard two voices raised in what sounded like a heated discussion. She thought that she recognized one of them as Rosella's. Thinking that it would be best if she checked in with her customer and let her know that the cookies had been delivered, she followed the sound of talking to a small room just off the main area. She knocked lightly on the door, and then knocked again harder when no one answered. The voices inside paused.

"I'll get it. It's probably the director of the funeral home," she heard the voice she thought was Rosella's say.

The door opened and the other woman looked at her, momentarily surprised. "It looks like you found the place okay. Thanks for delivering the cookies. This has been a crazy day. Do I need to give you a tip or anything for delivering them?"

"No, I was happy to do it," Lilah said.

"Well, thank you. People will begin to arrive soon. You're welcome to stay, if you want."

"I didn't really know him, and besides, I have to open the cookie shop," Lilah said. "I'm sure it will be lovely, though. And once again, I'm sorry for your loss."

She turned and was about to leave when she caught a glimpse of the person standing in the room behind Rosella. It was the guy with the brown hat. She froze, stunned. What was he doing here? She could believe a lot of things, but she couldn't believe that this was another coincidence. That man had been tied to Gunnar since day one, and it was obvious now that there was some sort of link between them.

"Is everything okay?" Rosella asked her.

Lilah tore her gaze away from the man, who was staring at his phone and hadn't seen her. "Yes, I'm fine. I'll be going now."

She turned and walked away, nearly running into a chair because her mind was elsewhere. She was trying to put the pieces together, but they just didn't make sense. How did the man with the brown hat know Rosella? How was he involved with Gunnar's death?

She couldn't leave these questions unanswered. She told herself it wasn't just because she wanted to satiate her own curiosity, but because Gunnar deserved to get justice for what had happened. She slipped into another small grieving room and took out her phone, pausing to consider her options. She didn't want to involve Margie in this, and while Val was her usual partner in crime, the other woman was still out of town. She knew that Reid would at least

KILLER VALENTINE COOKIES BOOK FIVE IN KILLER COOKIE COZY MYSTERIES

listen to what she had to say. He might be skeptical, but he wouldn't disbelieve her right off the bat.

She was disappointed when she reached his voicemail, mentally kicking herself. He was probably at work. The factory didn't shut down until tomorrow. It was only a few minutes away from the funeral home, so she left him a voicemail telling him what was going on. If he got a break, maybe he could come over and help her figure out what to do.

"What now?" She wanted to figure out who the man with the brown hat was, and how he knew Rosella. She was regretting not accepting the woman's invitation to stay. Was it too late? She could go back and tell her that she had changed her mind, and offer to help. If she walked away now, she would always wonder if she might have been on the verge of catching a killer. She knew she would regret it if she didn't act.

Feeling better now that she had decided to actually do something, she slipped out of the room only to come face-to-face with the man who owned the brown hat – though of course he wasn't wearing the hat now. He stared at her, shocked. He must have been so involved with his phone before that he hadn't realized that she was there.

"What are you doing here?" Lilah blurted out.

"I was about to ask you the same thing. Are you still following me?"

"No, I just brought the cookies for the wake."

"Oh." His face relaxed. "I remember Rosella mentioning something about that."

"What are you doing here?"

"Why do you care? I'm just helping Rosie set up. Not that it's any of your business."

"If you know Rosella, doesn't that mean that you would have known Gunnar? It didn't seem like the two of you knew each other in the cookie shop that day."

"What are you, the police?" he asked. "I didn't know Gunnar, I just know his sister. It was just a coincidence that I happened to be there at the same time that he was."

"Considering the size of the town, it's not that much of a coincidence at all." Rosella's voice came from behind her. Lilah jumped; she hadn't realized that the other woman had been nearby.

Rosella was staring at her with a sharp, calculating look on her face. Lilah realized that they outnumbered her, two to one, and she was essentially alone with them in the funeral home. She had no idea where the funeral homes director was, or if he would even hear if she called for help.

"Sorry to bother you guys," she said quickly, edging away from them. "I have to get going. Thanks for answering my questions."

Neither of them made a move to stop her, and she hurried down the hallway.

# CHAPTER THIRTEEN

She paused right after she turned the corner. Her heart was pounding, but she didn't want to leave yet. She still needed to find out what was going on.

She waited until she heard their voices fade away, then peeked around the corner to make sure the hallway was clear. She tiptoed forward, listening as hard as she could for Rosella's voice. If she could eavesdrop, then maybe she could figure out what was happening.

It wasn't difficult to find them. It sounded as if they were having an argument – rather, it sounded as if Rosella was criticizing her friend. Her voice was sharp with anger. Lilah stopped outside the door to the room where the wake was being held and pressed her ear against it. She could make out what they were saying, but just barely.

"How could you be so stupid, Billy? I told you not to be seen with him. Why did you think following him into the cookie shop was a good idea?"

"I was hungry, and the cookies looked good," Billy said. "I didn't think it would matter. There is no reason she would have connected the two of us. I didn't do anything to draw attention to myself."

"Really?" the other woman asked. "From the sound of it, she recognized you from more than just the cookie shop. What did you do?"

PATTI BENNING

"It's stupid," he muttered. "I needed to buy some energy drinks –"

"You know what? I don't even want to hear it. You chose the one woman who could place you near my brother the day he died, and you did something stupid to make yourself stand out. I should never have trusted you with this."

"Look, Rosie, you're making this sound worse than it –"

"Can I help you?" The deep voice came from behind Lilah. She spun around, backing into the door. When she realized it was just the funeral director, she breathed a sigh of relief.

"Sorry," she said, holding up her phone, which she had been gripping in her hand. "I was just texting someone to confirm the address of the next cookie delivery I have to make." It was a blatant lie, but it was the first thing that popped into her head.

"The wake will be starting soon, and we usually ask guests to make sure that their cell phones are on silent."

"I know. I'm sorry, I'll be leaving soon."

He left, and Lilah gave a sigh of relief. That had been a close one. She was on the verge of discovering what had happened to Gunnar, and by the sound of it, both Rosella and Billy had been involved.

She turned back to the door just as it opened. Rosella glared at her, then grabbed her by the arm and pulled her inside.

"We just can't get rid of you, can we?" she snapped.

"No, I was just walking by –"

"That's bull, and you know it. What did you hear?"

"Nothing, I promise."

"Shoot," Billy said. "Shoot, shoot, shoot. She probably heard everything."

"And who's fault is that?" Rosella asked, turning to glare at him.

"I told you I didn't think it would be a big deal. Stop blaming this on me. You're the one that wanted him dead. All of this is on you, and if it gets to the cops, I'll tell them about everything. I shouldn't have gotten dragged into this."

"Don't try to blame me for your mistake. You were happy enough to help me when I promised to pay you for it. If you had just done what I said and stayed back from him, we wouldn't be having this problem now."

"I don't understand what's going on," Lilah said.

"Shut up," Rosella told her. "And Billy, if you want to make things right, bring your truck around to the back of this place. Tell that director whatever you need to, just get it done. I want to get her out of here before people start arriving. My brother is going to have a nice wake, no matter what I have to do."

"I don't see why you care so much," Billy grumbled. "You're the one who wanted him dead, anyway. Who cares how his wake goes?"

"Billy," Rosella said in a dangerous voice. "Go get the truck. Now."

Lilah felt her phone buzz in her pocket. She reached for it automatically.

"Put your hands up and don't move," Rosella snapped as Billy slunk out the door.

Lilah began to comply, then stopped. Why was she doing what this woman told her to do? Now it was just the two of them, and Rosella might look dangerous, but she didn't have a weapon.

As if reading her mind, the other woman grabbed her purse and withdrew a small handgun. "I said, hands up."

Lilah did as she was told, her heart pounding. She was terrified and confused. Everything was happening so fast, and none of it made sense.

"Why did you want your brother dead?" she asked.

"Why should I tell you anything?"

"Well, we have to wait for Billy anyway, don't we? I don't know what you plan to do to me, but I can guess it's probably not very good. I just want to know why all this is happening."

"You wouldn't understand."

"Try me."

"My brother had terminal cancer. He had maybe six months to live, and he had just proposed to his fiancé, Mariah. If they got married before he died, all of that money he inherited – we're talking almost half a million dollars – would have gone to her. He had only known her for three months, for goodness sakes. I couldn't let him marry her, not with that much money on the table. Between my inheritance and what I would get from him, I would never have to work again. Why should someone who had only known him for three months get all of that money when I'm the one that spent every night caring for my grandparents as a child? I couldn't kill her, because I knew Gunnar would connect the dots. He's always been a smart one. Mariah… well, not so much."

"You killed your brother for money?" Lilah asked, feeling sick.

"I didn't kill anyone," Rosella said. "Billy did that for me. He's not the smartest guy, but he'll do whatever I tell him to, which is a plus. I shouldn't have trusted him for something like this, though. I'm not surprised he screwed it up."

"That's horrible," Lilah said. "How could you do something like that to your family?"

"I don't want to hear your judgment. Just shut your mouth and sit tight until Billy gets here with the truck. I'm done explaining myself to you."

Lilah didn't have a choice but to obey. The other woman had a gun, and even though Lilah didn't think that she would use it – a gun going off in a funeral home would certainly draw a lot of attention that the other woman wouldn't want – she wasn't about to risk getting shot to find out.

*That's another reason I shouldn't hire an employee,* she thought. *If I want something done right, it's best to do it myself.* She gave a dry laugh at the thought. Here she was thinking about employees when she was about ten minutes away from never even setting foot in the store again.

"Do you think this is funny? If I were you, I'd be keeping my mouth shut."

Lilah just looked at her, at a loss on how to reply. She felt like crying and screaming all at once. She hated being so helpless, but if this really was the end, she didn't want to go out sobbing on her knees. The last moments of her life shouldn't be spent crying.

She didn't want to go out at all. She shut her mouth tightly, glaring at Rosella and waiting for the other woman to make some sort of mistake so she could make her move. However, the gun that the other woman was holding pointed at her unwaveringly.

"Where is that boy?" Rosella muttered. "He should be around back by now. Don't move," she warned as she backed towards the exit on the other side of the room. She pushed it open a couple of inches and glanced out.

"The truck's here," she said. "I don't know why Billy didn't come in. Go on, you go out first. Move slowly and keep your hands up."

Lilah did as she was told, her palms sweaty. She walked toward the truck, her eyes roaming the parking lot. The truck was the only vehicle parked behind the building. No one else was here to offer her help.

"Get in the passenger side door, next to Billy. I'm not sure what we'll do with you yet, but you need to get out of here. Don't even think about –"

She broke off midway through her sentence. Lilah heard a thud, and then a clatter as something metallic fell to the pavement. She spun around to see Reid and Rosella struggling on the ground. The gun had fallen out of the other woman's grasp, and was only a few feet away from Lilah. She lunged forward and grabbed it, but didn't point at the struggling people on the ground. She was too afraid of hitting Reid.

"I have the gun, you can let her go," she said instead. Reid looked over his shoulder and saw her holding the firearm. He got up quickly, backing away from Rosella, who was fuming.

"It's over," he said to her. "I called the police as soon as I recognized him –" he jerked his head toward the truck behind them, "– in the parking lot out front. Between seeing him and getting your voicemail, I knew that you had managed to get yourself in trouble once again. Though I have to admit, I wasn't expecting to see you at gunpoint." He turned to her, looking her up and down. "Are you okay?"

"I'm fine," she said. She realized she was still holding the gun awkwardly, and handed it over to him. "Here, I don't trust myself with this. What now?"

"Now," he said, "we wait for the police to get here and put them behind bars, where they can't hurt anyone else."

# EPILOGUE

Lilah turned on her kitchen light and greeted a frantic Winnie as she walked in the door. The instant the beagle saw who was behind her, she darted around her legs. While Reid was petting the dog, Lilah put a kettle of water on the stove. Tea sounded perfect just then.

"Do you want me to get going?" Reid asked from behind her.

"No," she said. "I mean, if you want to. But if you wanted to stay for a bit… that would be fine."

She reached for a mug, but somehow it slipped through her fingers and shattered on the counter. Suddenly Reid's arms were around her. She leaned into him and closed her eyes.

"It's been a rough day," he said. "You should go sit down. I'll make the tea and let Winnie outside."

She wanted to protest, but instead found herself nodding. "Thank you," she said. "I don't know what's wrong with me. I feel shaky."

"Someone pointed a gun at you today," he said. "I don't blame you for being a little unsteady."

"I just can't believe how close it was. If you hadn't been there –"

"I was," he said. "What might have happened doesn't matter. It didn't happen, that's what's important. I won't let anyone hurt you."

"But they could have hurt *you*," she said. "I love you. I don't want –"

She broke off, realizing what she had said. It had slipped out, and had felt completely natural, just like Margie had said.

"Maybe we should continue this conversation another time," Reid said. Her face was still buried in his shoulder so she couldn't see his expression, but she thought she could tell by his voice that he was smiling. "I don't want you to say anything you'll regret later."

"I mean it," she said, pulling away slightly so she could look up at him. "I don't know why it took me so long to realize it, but this past week, spending time with you again… it made me realize how perfect everything is when we're together. I've never been in a relationship like this before, and I think I was scared by the thought of how much you mean to me, but today made me realize how wrong I was. I shouldn't be scared of how I feel. If one of us had gotten killed today, I might never have had the chance to say it back to you. And *that's* a scary thought."

He looked into her eyes for a long moment, and then, he kissed her. Despite everything that had happened that day, her heart lifted. She still didn't know what the future might bring, or where the two of them would find themselves in five years, but in that moment, it didn't matter.

"Go sit down," he said at last. "I'll bring the tea. You're still shaking."

She left him in the kitchen and sat down on the couch, too full of emotion to say anything else. She stroked Oscar, who had settled down on top of her lap, and realized it was still Valentine's Day. It may not have gone exactly as she had planned, but she had gotten her romantic holiday after all.

Made in the USA
Monee, IL
20 February 2022

91548861R00089